This book belongs to:

_____

_____

·GRANDPA CUTLASS·

THIS IS A BORZOI BOOK PUBLISHED BY ALFRED A. KNOPF

Copyright © 2011 by Hannah Shaw

Visit us on the Web! www.randomhouse.com/kids

Educators and librarians, for a variety of teaching tools,
visit us at www.randomhouse.com/teachers

Library of Congress Cataloging-in-Publication Data
Shaw, Hannah.
School for bandits / by Hannah Shaw.
p. cm.
Summary: Ralph Raccoon is too polite, so his parents send him
to Bandit School to learn to behave like a properly bad raccoon.
ISBN 978-0-375-86768-2 (trade) — ISBN 978-0-375-96768-9 (lib. bdg.)
[1. Raccoons—Fiction. 2. Etiquette—Fiction. 3. Behavior—Fiction.] I. Title.
PZ7.S534227Sc 2011
[E]—dc22
2010039516
The illustrations in this book were created using a combination of pen and ink,
printmaking techniques, and Photoshop.
MANUFACTURED IN CHINA
November 2011
10 9 8 7 6 5 4 3 2 1   First American Edition
Random House Children's Books supports the First Amendment and celebrates the right to read.

To Imi,
my sister in crime,
& winsome Betsy
the flapjack bandit!

·UNCLE WHISKERS·

SCHOOL
for
BANDITS

MRS RACCOON · RALPH · MR RACCOON

HANNAH SHAW

Alfred A. Knopf · New York

Mr. and Mrs. Raccoon were worried about their son, Ralph.

He *looked* perfectly normal,

BUT . . .

. . . he didn't act normal at all.

He was disturbingly
well behaved,

clean and tidy,

and he even
brushed his teeth.

THROW YOUR FOOD!

He didn't like lunchtime either,

or the sports activities that everyone else was so enthusiastic about.

The first week at school
was one disaster after another.

He failed the science test.

He failed art.

And he failed to impress Mrs. Mischief.

"Ralph Raccoon!
You MUST learn to take
things that aren't yours
WITHOUT asking,"
she scolded.

At the end of the term, Mrs. Mischief
gave Ralph his report card to take home.

"Not much improvement,"
she said with a frown.

REPORT
RALPH RACCOON
very well
BEHAVED.
FAR too
POLITE.

Then she gave them each a big sack.

"Whoever fills their sack with the most loot during the vacation will win the BEST BANDIT IN SCHOOL competition. Good luck, everyone!"

Ralph's loot sack stayed empty throughout the school vacation.

Meanwhile, all the other raccoons were busy trying to fill theirs.

"Don't you want to go and play?" asked his mum.

Ralph shook his head: he didn't want to cause trouble.

On the first day of the new term, Ralph picked up his empty sack with a heavy heart and started to walk to school.

It just didn't seem *right* to try and win a competition by being really bad.

Ralph was so deep in thought that he almost bumped into a flustered-looking poodle.

TREATS

Library

Grooming Parlor

5

PET STORE

GROOMING

PARK

LOOT

"What a lovely young raccoon," said the poodle, and gave him pawfuls of sticky sweets.

"Excuse me, can I help you?" asked Ralph politely.

"My HAIR!" she wailed. "It's a disaster!"

Ralph pointed her in the direction of the grooming parlor.

He put the sweets in his sack and walked on.

LOOT

PARK

As he crossed the park,
he gave a friendly wave
to a family having a picnic.

But something wasn't right.
They were jumping
up and down, shouting:
"Fluffy!
Come down!"

Poor Fluffy was clinging helplessly to a tree.
Quickly Ralph climbed up to rescue her.

"How kind!" said the family,
and they gave Ralph
lots of yummy goodies
from their picnic hamper.

Ralph put the goodies
in his sack and walked on.

As he strolled
past the bandstand,
Ralph noticed it was empty.

He spotted the entire brass band
standing at the edge of the duck pond.

They weren't playing
their usual happy tunes.

"What's wrong?"
asked Ralph.

"Our music blew into the pond!"
wailed the conductor.

"Don't worry!"
said Ralph. "I'll get it!"

And he swam out to fetch it.

"What a hero," tooted the band,
and they loaded Ralph
with armfuls of treats.

He gratefully added the treats
to his collection and turned toward school.

By now the sack was so heavy,
Ralph could hardly lift it.
With much tugging and struggling,
he dragged it into the classroom.

The other bigger, bolder,
much badder raccoons
stared in astonishment.

Not one of them had
done nearly as well.

"Well done, Ralph!" said a rather surprised-looking Mrs. Mischief.

"You've won the BEST BANDIT IN SCHOOL competition!"

Ralph had his photo taken, and Mrs. Mischief told his proud parents, who couldn't stop smiling.

"Just like his Grandpa Cutlass," said his dad, beaming.

The other raccoons were puzzled
and just a little bit jealous.

"Tell us how you did it,"
they begged. . . .

Ralph grinned at his new friends.

"Well, first you have to say
'Please....'"

And that's just what they did.